14.99

for Katie Randall and Virgil
with love

PUBLISHED BY DOUBLEDAY
a division of Bantam Doubleday Dell Publishing Group, Inc.
666 Fifth Avenue, New York, New York, 10103

DOUBLEDAY
and the portrayal of an anchor with a dolphin
are trademarks of Doubleday, a division of
Bantam Doubleday Dell Publishing Group, Inc.

Originally published in England by Faber and Faber Ltd.

Library of Congress Cataloging-in-Publication Data applied for

ISBN 0–385–41843–4
ISBN 0–385–41844–2 (lib. bdg.)

PRINTED IN BELGIUM
JUNE 1991
FIRST EDITION IN THE UNITED STATES OF AMERICA

DEAREST
GRANDMAMA

WRITTEN AND ILLUSTRATED

BY

CATHERINE BRIGHTON

DOUBLEDAY

NEW YORK LONDON TORONTO SYDNEY AUCKLAND

1 November 1830   *Meralda*, at sea

Dearest Grandmama,

    It is a whole year since I left. I do hope you
received my letters from Africa and you liked my
funny drawings. All these letters will be posted on to
you when we reach our next landfall.

    Today I am tying labels on the shells that
Papa has found. Down in the dark hold Papa
keeps the creatures he has captured in big crates. Mr.
Tubbs, the ship's cook, lets me feed them if I am
really careful. Mr. Snaughty has cut my lovely hair!
I know you will not mind because it is getting in
the way when I go swimming. Yes, I can swim!
Well, nearly.

                    Your loving granddaughter,
                    Maudie-Ann

7 November 1830   *Meralda*, at sea

Dearest Grandmama,

    This evening I went wandering along the
ship's rail. I was looking over the side into the dark
sea when I saw a boy climbing out of a small boat.
He was climbing up on to the *Meralda*! The crew were
too busy singing to hear my calling so I helped him
up myself. He never said a word as I took him past
the singing sailors and down to the cabins. Mr. Tubbs
gave me some food but the silent boy just pushed it
away. What kind of boy is it, Grandmama, who
comes from nowhere and does not eat or speak?

            Your loving granddaughter,
              Maudie-Ann

8 November 1830   *Meralda*, at sea

Dearest Grandmama,

I have found some clothes for the silent boy.

As I hung the boy's raggedy jacket on the door,
Grandmama, a letter dropped out. I remember my
dear departed mama telling me not to read other
people's letters but without thinking, I am afraid,
I read it, Grandmama.

It said:

"Dear Dr. Estepona,

This is the boy I spoke of in my last letter. I
am sending him to you from the port of New York
in the care of the captain of the *Marie Celeste*.

As I explained, he has not spoken for three
years now and I have done all I can. I hope most
sincerely that your new methods might help him.

Yours very sincerely,
Dr. Alban Bishop"

But Grandmama, the letter was dated 1872,
forty years into the future!

When the silent boy was dressed I took
him to Papa's mirror to show him how smart
he looked. I stared and stared, Grandmama, but
I could only see myself! He had *no reflection*! I
got very angry and shook him and turned him
around and still there was no reflection.

What kind of boy is it, Grandmama, who
does not have a reflection?

Your loving granddaughter,
Maudie-Ann

11 November 1830   *Meralda*, at sea

Dearest Grandmama,

    This morning I took the silent boy to Papa's
laboratory where we keep the specimens. It smells
of chemicals but he didn't mind. I showed him the
stuffed birds that stare down from every shelf and the
skeletons that rattle when the *Meralda* sways. But
then he heard the ship's clock and he covered his ears
and turned away. I closed the lid and because he
still looked frightened I turned the tiny key.

    "Look," I said, "I've locked it. I have made
time stand still."

    After that he smiled and we sat at Papa's
desk and I showed him the shells. But what kind
of boy is it, Grandmama, who is frightened of
time?

                    Your loving granddaughter,
                         Maudie-Ann

14 November 1830   *Meralda*, at sea

Dearest Grandmama,

　　We have had a bad storm and the *Meralda* has been tossed by huge waves. Papa was worried about the creatures in the hold because the crates were breaking up.

　　I hung on tight, Grandmama, as the sea rolled across the deck. I shall never forget what I saw when my eyes cleared. One of Papa's creatures, a thing he calls a "crocodile," was coming toward me! As I ran to escape, another wave swept me toward the edge of the ship. If the silent boy had not been there to grab me I would surely have drowned in the thundering waves. What kind of boy is it, Grandmama, who is not afraid of dying in the angry sea?

　　　　　Your loving granddaughter,
　　　　　Maudie-Ann

20 November 1830   *Meralda*, at anchor

Dearest Grandmama,

    The weather is very different now.

    The sun is baking hot and every now and then a
tiny breeze ruffles a sail. The *Meralda* has passed into
calmer waters and we are anchored among
some small islands. When we look over the side the
silent boy and I can see thousands of brightly
colored fish darting between the rocks. When I look
at my reflection in the smooth surface of the sea I am
alone. There is no reflection of the boy.

    Papa has decided to explore the islands because
there will be plants and creatures that he has never seen.

The crew lowered the boats, and we all climbed in and rowed to the island. A tropical island, Grandmama, is not much like home. There are huge butterflies and monkeys that hide in the trees. They threw coconuts down and one hit the silent boy but, Grandmama, he did not even notice.

What kind of boy is it, Grandmama, who does not feel pain?

Your loving granddaughter,
Maudie-Ann

21 November 1830   *Meralda*, at anchor

Dearest Grandmama,

While Papa was searching the island for
specimens, the silent boy and I returned to the beach.
We trailed our hands in the rock pools and watched
the tiny fish darting away. Under our feet the
sand was littered with shells and I noticed the
silent boy was collecting them and putting them in
his pocket.

The hot sun beat down on the sand as I
fished for Blue Tangs, and as I looked at the silent
boy threading his shells, I realized that he did not
have a shadow.

Later in the afternoon, when we were climbing in
the rigging, the silent boy gave me his string of shells
to wear around my neck. As the sky turned from blue
to purple and the sun was beginning to set I turned
to the silent boy and said,

"Look, the sun is sinking!"

And then, Grandmama, the boy turned to me and *spoke*!

He repeated my word!

"Sinking! Sinking! Sinking!" But that was all he said.

What kind of boy is it, Grandmama, who has
only one word and that word is "sinking"?

I have left the silent boy up in the rigging
watching the sun setting.

Your loving granddaughter,
Maudie-Ann

22 November 1830   *Meralda*, at sea

Dearest Grandmama,

    I am so sad I can hardly write.

    The silent boy has gone. When I awoke this
morning he was nowhere in sight. I ran up and down
the deck calling. I thought he was hiding. The crew
looked confused and called for Papa. He carried me,
kicking and struggling, to his cabin.

    ''What is the matter, Maudie-Ann?'' he asked.
I told him the silent boy had gone.

    And then, Grandmama, do you know what Papa said?

    He said, ''What boy, Maudie-Ann? There was no boy.''

    ''But, Papa! The silent boy! The boy with no
shadow and no reflection! The boy who could feel no
pain and only said 'sinking!' ''

    I was crying, Grandmama.

    ''You must have imagined it,'' said Papa, and
he made me lie down.

    Oh, Grandmama, I did not just imagine him.

                Your sad, sad, granddaughter,
                   Maudie-Ann

4 December 1830

Hotel de los Vistas
Rio de Janeiro
Brazil

Dear Mother,

I am afraid Maudie-Ann has not been very well.

I think it is due to the heat. However, I may not have paid her enough attention.

She became very upset the other day because she claimed she had a little friend from the future and he had disappeared! She says he came from a boat called the *Marie Celeste*. I even checked in the Registry of Ships to show her no such vessel exists.

I have taken Maudie-Ann shopping in Rio and saw some interesting sights. She seems much happier now and is looking forward to the next part of the voyage. I have sent her letters on to you and she will write again soon, but she asked me to tell you she has a charming string of shells.

Your devoted son,
Edgar

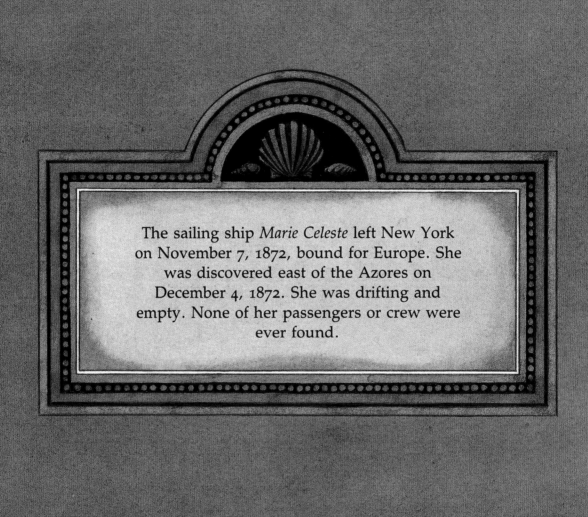

The sailing ship *Marie Celeste* left New York on November 7, 1872, bound for Europe. She was discovered east of the Azores on December 4, 1872. She was drifting and empty. None of her passengers or crew were ever found.

F
Bri

Brighton
Dearest Grandmama

DATE DUE			
OCT 18		OCT 18	
DEC 06		DEC 6 1993	
8	FEB 8 1994	FEB 8	
	MAR 1 6		
		SEP 05	
DEC 16 1994	OCT 27	MAY 17